# The Perfect Raindrop

## Written and Illustrated

## By

## Sharon Lee Levine

PerfectRaindrop1@aol.com

Meow Ideas

ISBN 978-0-578-00737-3

A special story
of
everlasting friendship.

Once upon a time while I was wandering around in my backyard I saw a beam of light come out of the sky and a lady stepped out of the beam.

She wore a big headdress, she had very large eyes, and she was very tall.

She asked if I wanted to go on a journey.

So I stepped into the beam
and

away we went...

The next thing I knew I was stepping out of the beam...



Somewhere else.



That's when I first saw him.
He was kneeling by some water and colors were swirling all around him.

Despite all the activity
the little being was extremely
serene in his task.

I felt serene as well and I asked him
how he turned the water into
all those beautiful colors.

He told me it came from the magic
of the
mind and spirit.

He said he had a mission to go on
and asked if I wanted to go.


It's about water he said,
some planets need more water.


And I'm searching for the perfect raindrop.

Once I find the perfect raindrop
I'll bring it back with me.


Then I'll let it multiply to lots of raindrops.


That's what I was doing when you first saw me.

During our search we traveled to wondrous
falls...
And took in the surroundings.

We walked through woods.

Floated down a river.

And sat among the stars.

We spoke without speaking.
He put his thoughts to my mind.

And I put my thoughts to his.

I learned to use more of my mind...

By exploring the world...

Of my subconscious.

We even traveled back to my planet.

You have the most beautiful planet
he told me.
Despite all the violence we still
like coming here.

It's still new, still learning and
still having tantrums.

I told him he seemed familiar.
He told me he had been all over and that
I          had been too.

When your body         vessel wears out
your mind spirit takes off on a wondrous
journey
to other places and times.

Or it may stay put.
Our mind spirits have been jumping all over
the place.

The reason we don't fully remember

is we don't always remember all our yesterdays.


He told me I'm living on a pretty new planet

right now.

And things can get pretty confusing here.

As they get calmer I'll remember more.

He brought me to the planet in need of the
raindrop.
And told me...

Once there was a raging ocean here
swirling in every direction
tossing seashells high in the air.

The ocean slowly dried into thirty two lakes.
Into a pattern which now means...


You will never know anything
Like the loss of
Your planets water.


In the night sky
It reflects
On the full moon...

Sometimes we would lie in the fields...

And look at the moons.

I met his friends.

And he met mine.
They weren't all that different.

On our travels we met a beautiful lady with
eleven braids of hair flowing freely
from her head.

She told us nine of the braids represented
nine planets in the earth's solar system.

And another was for the sun
and another for the moon.

She said the earth's solar system was a very
balanced place.
Which was why she chose to represent it
with her hair.

And someday may earth be the same.

I learned to watch myself.

We traveled to a planet
where we watched the sunrise
through the trees.


And there we found it,
sitting on a leaf
after the morning rain...

The Perfect Raindrop.

So now my friend bids me a farewell
and I to him.


Perhaps our mind spirits will meet again
in another galaxy.
Or right here in this one.

I wonder what our life forms will be,
and if there will be that important
glimpse of recognition.



With a friendship as important as this...


I know there will.

Thank you and goodbye.

Sharon Lee Levine is an actress, writer and artist.
The Perfect Raindrop is her first book.
And she does not believe in eating animals.